Believe in Fall

AMY SPARLING

Believe in Fall

CHAPTER
ONE

Keanna

It's a beautiful Texas day. Well, as beautiful as it can get in the middle of August. The sun is beating down on us as if its only goal in life is to tan everyone to a crisp. But even though it's hotter than Hades outside, it's still a pretty day. A day that shouldn't be spent in the stuffy library of the local community college, surrounded by people who would all clearly rather be somewhere else.

I gaze at the long line ahead of me. It's amazing how many people don't know how to use a freaking computer. I would be at home today, among the people who *do* know how to use a computer, if some utility worker hadn't made an epic screw up.

Early in the morning, while messing with the cables that run underground, some guy from the cable company accidentally severed the lines that bring internet to our apart of the town. My parents got an email (ironically, which they had to read on their cell phones) apologizing for the inconvenience and saying they hope to have internet restored by next week.

Next week will be too late to register for college classes. Next week doesn't help me at all.

I tried registering for classes on my phone, but the website is not made for that, and it just didn't work. So, I had to do what my mom called the old school thing, and head up to the college during one of their registration days. That means standing in long lines to talk to a counselor who will help you fill out a paper with the classes you want to register for. Then you have to take that paper to the admissions office and pay tuition. Last semester, I did it all online in just a few minutes, all from the comfort of my pajamas.

It's like the freaking stone ages in here. I chuckle to myself as I gaze around at the twenty or so people standing ahead of me. We're sectioned off by last names, and the H through P section is the longest. Go figure. It doesn't escape my notice that most of the people in these lines are older, people in their forties and so who are going back to college. I guess they still prefer doing things the manual way.

I send a text to Jett to pass the boredom.

Me: I miss technology.

Jett: You're using technology right now...

Me: I miss the internet...at my home...

Jett: Are you still at the college?

Me: Yep...waiting in line to register.

Jett: that sucks. I'm almost home...I figured you'd be home too.

Jett had left bright and early this morning to pick up his dirt bike from the only shop around that does the best suspension work. It's nearly in Houston, so it was a long drive. I glance at the time—11:15, and realize I've been here for over an hour.

Me: Help me...this line is never ending

Jett: I'll drop off my bike and head your way

I smile. Sure, I feel a little guilty for making Jett come up here just to keep me company, but that's what boyfriends do. His only other plans today were to ride his dirt bike, and you can ride a dirt bike any time of day. There's only a few hours you get to stand in line with your girlfriend, being bored out of your mind. Ha!

By the time he gets here, there's only two people ahead of me, and both of them turn to watch Jett walk up. He's a force of sexuality, that boy. Wearing black shorts, Adidas shoes, and a Team Loco blue T-shirt, he looks just as good as he smells.

"Hi babe," he says, sliding an arm around my waist as he presses a kiss to my cheek. "This line isn't long at all."

I smack him on the chest. "That's because I've already been waiting for hours."

He grins and takes the brochure from my hand, thumbing through the dog-eared pages. "So, what classes are you signing up for?"

"Just basic stuff. History, Government, English, a stupid PE class called Powerwalking." I shrug. "The core stuff. Luckily I have another year of basic classes before I need to figure out what I want to study."

"It's weird," Jett says, handing the brochure back to me. His lips slide to the side of his mouth as he thinks. "I'm like...a little jealous? But mostly not. I mean, you're in college and that's awesome, and I kind of want to be in college, but I'd rather ride a bike for a living, you know?"

He grins at me in this horribly cute way that still makes my toes tingle after all this time.

"Yeah well college is what normal people do. The people without crazy dirt bike skills."

"Are you ready to register?" The woman behind the table's voice startles me. I can't believe I'm already at the front of the line. Being with Jett always makes the time go by faster. I should bring him with me every time I have to wait for something.

When I'm officially signed up for classes, we take my registration papers to the school bookstore so I can get all the textbooks I'll need. Jett looks around in wonder as we trek across the school campus, sticking to the sidewalks that link all of the buildings together even though most people just cut through the grass.

"This place is pretty cool," he says. He steps to the side so a guy walking toward us can get by, then he moves back to standing next to me. "It's like how colleges are in the movies. All these people with backpacks and laptops, walking around being all hip and millennial."

I snort out a laugh. "You're such a dork. *We* are millennials, you know that right?"

"Yeah, but we're cooler than most people. Hey, look at that!" He points toward the art building where large sculptures are set up on display in the courtyard. His eyes go wide. "It's fancy art. How very collegiate."

I roll my eyes. "This is just a community college, you know. The bigger universities are probably a million times cooler than this place."

"I didn't really want to go to college, but being here is making me change my mind."

"Wait until you see all the homework and essays I

have to write after the semester starts. You'll change your mind again."

"Yeah, I forgot about that," he says, curling his lip in disgust.

We reach the bookstore, which is a large circular building with a domed ceiling that's mostly skylights. It was built in the eighties so it smells like musty old building in here, but it's still pretty cool. A blast of cold air conditioning hits me as I walk inside with Jett right behind me.

Smooth jazz music plays overhead and the two students working behind the counter are sporting several tattoos and LCC college shirts.

"Babe!" Jett says playfully as he wanders over to a rack of those LCC shirts. "Why don't you have any of this awesome merch?" He holds up a hot pink shirt with the school's logo on the front.

I roll my eyes and shove his hand away. "Because I don't have any school spirit, that's why."

"We're going to change that," he says, taking the pink shirt off the hanger and then reaching for a lime green one. "You're my college girl now, and you should be proud." He throws the shirts over his shoulder and then moves to a rack of LCC school supplies.

Yeah, all of the school stuff is kind of cool, but I've never bought any because all the people I see at the motocross track always wear *real* college stuff. Like state universities, or ivy league schools. Community college feels so lame.

When I think back to being raised by my biological mother and how we were nothing but white trash, I do feel proud that I'm enrolled in at least some college, even though it's not a fancy one. Maybe I do need a shirt.

Jett follows me toward the book section, his arms loaded down with silly LCC things he thinks I need. We go through the list of my four classes this semester and find all the books I'll need.

The total comes to just over five hundred dollars, but luckily, I have a scholarship for a thousand dollars that I earned from a local electric company. All I had to do was write an essay on why I loved Lawson, Texas. Since Lawson is the town that gave me my new parents, my boyfriend, and my future, it was pretty easy to write.

Jett insists on buying the LCC stuff for me, and one of the cashiers can't seem to keep her eyes off him. I've seen that look in girls' eyes before. They think he's hot and they can't help but stare. It used to make me jealous, but now it makes me feel kind of awesome. Jett is the guy every girl wants, and yet he's all mine.

What's even cuter is that if a girl isn't actively flirting with him, he doesn't even notice it. I guess if you're crazy hot, maybe you get used to people gawking at you nonstop.

Jett carries my books and shopping bag in one hand and throws the other one over my shoulder as we make our way back out to the parking lot. "Have I ever told you how amazingly beautiful you are?" he asks.

I give him a sarcastic look. "Maybe once or twice."

"Well, you are. I'm so lucky to have you."

I just grin like an idiot at that comment. Jett has been in an amazing mood ever since his summer race series ended with him taking the first place trophy. He and the other three rookie guys from Team Loco raced in this ten week summer series that took place all over the nation. There were twenty other racers as well, some of them on professional motocross teams like Jett, and some were just private racers hoping for their lucky break. Out of all ten races, they average up everyone's stats, and although Jett ended up taking second place two times, he still got first place overall. Another guy from Team Loco named Clay Summers took second place overall and then Aiden Strauss was third place. It was the first time a single professional race team had their own riders on the podium, so it was a big win for Team Loco in general.

I'll never forget the look on Jett's face at that last race in California, when he stepped up on the podium and they handed him the first place trophy. I've never seen him smile so big, and I've never been so proud in my life.

Now he gets the rookie position on the professional arenacross races this year. The season starts in a couple of weeks and his other Team Loco rookies will be there to cheer him on. As much as I loved traveling with Jett for the last four races of the summer season, now that college is starting, I'll only be able to go to the races that are close by. Luckily, arenacross comes to Houston, San Antonio, and Dallas this season. I'm going to be at every one, cheering him on as he pursues his dreams.

CHAPTER
TWO

Jett

Arenacross is a whole different beast from motocross, which is held outside on an open track. It's even different from supercross, which is inside a stadium. They're similar, but arenacross is small. Very small. A tight track with lots of jumps and hardly any room to move around. They're usually held in smaller stadiums, like the one happening this weekend in San Antonio, Texas. There aren't any arenacross tracks at home to practice on, and since most of them are built specifically for one race and then demolished so the stadium can host concerts and stuff, I never get to practice.

I'm not going to say I'm nervous, exactly. I'm just a little ready to get this over with.

My ultimate goal is to race in the actual AMA Motocross seasons. That's the most professional of professional that you can get. Right now, I still have to race these smaller things and prove myself worthy to my team. Team Loco has a dozen other riders who are in their twenties and thirties who come from all over the world, and most of them can probably kick my ass on the track. Dad tells me not to worry about it because I'll get there eventually. I'm confident that I will, but I have to put up with these smaller pro races first.

I throw my suitcase onto my bed and find two old socks left over in there from when I used it last time. Gross. I toss them into the dirty laundry hamper and then get to work packing up for two days in San Antonio. It's only a few hours away, so Keanna and I decided to drive. Airplanes get stuffy and old after a while. I'd way rather spend three hours in my truck alone with Keanna than forty five minutes in a plane with strangers.

When all my stuff is packed, I haul it downstairs and set it by the back door so I'll be ready to go at nine in the morning. My mom is hosting family dinner tonight to say goodbye to us, even though we're only going to be gone for two freaking days. She's making lasagna though, so I'm not going to complain.

When Keanna comes over for dinner, her parents and little brother are with her. Her parents, Becca and Park, are best friends with my parents. Most of the time this is a great thing because they're all pretty chill as far as parents go.

Other times it can be totally embarrassing.

"There's my future son-in-law," Becca says as she walks by. She ruffles my hair, which is something she's done to me ever since I was a little kid. But now that I'm six feet tall and she's still five foot three, it kind of loses it's meaning because she has to reach up so high.

I tell her hello and I ignore the future son-in-law comment. They always do that—act like we're getting married soon, or sometimes like we already are married. I love Keanna with all of my heart and when I gave her that promise ring that she wears on her left hand, I knew one day it'd be switched out with an engagement ring.

But having your parents talk about it all the time is a little annoying. I know they're just happy for us, but I don't ever want our relationship to feel like something that's been laid out for us without our input. When I officially propose to Keanna, I want it to be because *we* chose to take that step in our lives, not because we feel obligated to.

"Hey," I say, reaching out and brushing my fingers down Keanna's arm.

She gives me this exasperated smile, and it's probably because of what her mom just said.

We all sit around the dining table: my parents, Keanna's parents, our little siblings, and us. Mom's lasagna is delicious as always, and my baby sister Brooke, who is only four months old, looks at it like she wishes she could eat some instead of drinking her bottle.

Keanna's brother Elijah is old enough to eat it, but he makes more of a mess with his food in his high chair that actually eating it.

The parents talk about whatever, and Keanna and I kind of split into our own world. We sit close together at the end of the table, my leg touching hers, my elbow brushing against hers as we eat.

It seems to take forever, but finally dinner is over. The parents all tell me good luck at my races this weekend, and I thank them and then drag Keanna upstairs to my room for some privacy.

Keanna didn't allow us to stay up too late last night since we have to wake up early today, but I still feel like shit when my alarm goes off. My girlfriend is up and ready though, bouncing off my bed as if she's been infused with the sunshine that's filtering in from my blinds.

"No..." I say, rolling over in bed and hitting snooze on my phone's alarm. "Five more minutes."

"Babe!" Keanna says, walking over to my side of the bed. It'd taken only a little bit of begging on my part to get her to spend the night last night. She looks hot as hell wearing my T-shirt over her panties. She puts her hands on her hips. "You said if we leave by eight-thirty then we'll have time to get bagels."

"I did say that," I say, pulling the pillow over my head. I take a deep breath and then sit up even though all I want to do is sleep some more.

There's this bagel place on the outskirts of town and they sell New York style bagels that are freaking amazing. But the line is always long so it's hard to stop on our way if we don't have time to waste.

Keanna brushes her teeth while I get dressed, and I watch her from the reflection in the bathroom mirror. She's wearing shorts and a tank top but she looks adorable. I love her in a ponytail. She always looks so happy and carefree when she hasn't put much time into her looks. When we're forced to dress up for some formal event or dinner, she always tends to freak out and worry about herself all night. Telling her how beautiful she is doesn't ever help.

But on days like today, where all we have to do is

drive to San Antonio and check into our hotel, she doesn't stress too much.

There's a heat race tonight, which isn't that big of a deal. It's basically a qualifier race to determine who makes it into the official race tomorrow. They only allow twenty five racers and about seventy five show up to qualify. That starts at six this evening, so we've got all day.

My mom is downstairs with the baby and she offers us coffee, but we decline because the bagel place has amazing coffee. I kiss my little sister Brooke goodbye and she touches my face with a drool-covered little hand.

"Thanks," I say, rubbing my cheek on my sleeve.

"It means she loves you," Mom says.

"Uh huh. Sure."

Mom hugs Keanna and me goodbye and then we're finally on the road. There's nothing better than driving in my truck with my girl by my side.

I reach over and grab her thigh, but she doesn't acknowledge me because she's on her phone. I slide my hand up and squeeze right above her knee where it tickles.

That works.

"Ahh!" she squeals, swatting at my hand.

"Whatcha doing?" I ask.

She scrolls down the screen on her phone. "Just

reading all your fan messages on Facebook," she says with a laugh. "San Antonio loves you."

"Well—" I say, starting to make some funny joke, but she interrupts me.

"You didn't let me finish," she says, sticking out her tongue. It's so sexy, I'd reach over there and bite it if I wasn't driving. She looks back at her phone. "They love you in San Antonio, but they might love Clay more."

I scoff. "That tatted up stone wall? Why would they like him? He hates everyone."

She shrugs. "That's probably why. You're too nice to everyone and you have this kind boy next door vibe. Clay is edgy and kind of a dick, and girls like that."

I give her a look.

"*Some* girls," she says. "Not me. I like the sweet guy next door."

"Good thing I am literally next door," I say, winking.

I like my teammate Clay, and he's going to this race as a backup for Team Loco. Where I have a life and a girlfriend and I help my family run the Track part time, Clay only focuses on dirt bikes. It's kind of creepy how focused he is. But it didn't help him win the summer race, and I know he's been aching to prove himself ever since.

"Maybe the girls need to like him more," I say as we drive down an empty I-10 toward the bagel shop. "He needs something to distract him from dirt bikes, just a little. Enough to make him loosen up a bit."

"Why, so you can keep beating him?" she says with a smirk.

"No..." I grin. "Okay, maybe."

Our hotel is a Hilton that's only a few blocks away from the Alamo, and after the races are over tomorrow, I'm going to make sure we stop by and see it. Clay hasn't checked in yet, and Marcus won't get here until his plane lands around four, so I don't feel guilty spending the first few hours of my racing weekend with my girlfriend.

We head outside to the pool and swim around a bit, and then wander into the hotel's restaurant and order some lunch.

"Can we eat this upstairs?" Keanna says after we place our order. She chews on her thumbnail.

"Sure. Are you okay?"

She shrugs. "Those girls are looking at you and pointing at you and I'm pretty sure they're trying to get the courage to come talk to you."

I don't look back to where the girls sit so as not to give them ammunition. I know it makes her uncomfortable to have other girls talk to me in public.

"I think all the arenacross people are staying in this hotel, so it makes sense that I'd get recognized here."

Her lips slide into a thin smile. "It's fine. It's just... ugh."

"I get it, babe." I flag the waiter down. "Is there any way we can get our food delivered to our room instead?"

"Of course," he says, beaming at me with a toothy grin.

"No, that's okay," Keanna says. "It's fine. We don't have to run away just because you're popular."

"I don't mind," I tell her. Our waiter watches me questioningly, waiting for confirmation on what he should do. "We'll take it to go."

"Are you sure?" Keanna says. Now she looks worried and guilty, and all those other emotions that make her chew on her thumbnail.

I give her a heartwarming smile. "I'm positive. Let's go."

I make sure to take her hand as soon as we leave, in case any of those girls are watching. I know it should be common knowledge by now that *Jett Adams Has A Girlfriend*, but some people still don't know, or they choose not to care.

It is kind of cool getting all this attention from girls and guys and everyone now that I'm mildly famous in the motocross world, but I'd never want Keanna to feel threatened.

Our dinner is pretty amazing, but I don't eat too

much or else I'll puke out on the track tonight. After eating and watching some TV, I get a text from Marcus to meet him down at the arena next door. Practice starts in half an hour and then the heat race will start promptly at seven.

"Could I maybe stay here while you practice?" Keanna says. She peers up at me from the hotel bed with puppy dog eyes. "It's just that I have to be there all alone when you're riding and it gets boring. I'd rather just go there right before the official race starts."

I laugh because I can tell it took a lot of guts for her to ask that. "Of course," I say, leaning down and kissing her. "Let me get your pass."

I'm already digging in my suitcase for my lucky underwear, so I reach for the VIP pass Marcus sent me for Keanna and me. Mine says I'm a racer and hers says she part of the pit crew. It's a slight lie, but that's the only way to get anyone access to the pit area of the stadium, otherwise she'd have to stay up in the stands with everyone else.

"Here's your pass," I say, handing her the laminated card strung on a lanyard. "Do you know where my lucky underwear are?"

She frowns. "Did you remember to get them out of the dryer?"

"Dammit." I cover my face with my hands and look up at the ceiling. "No. *Shit.*"

"Baby, you'll be fine," she assures me. "Underwear doesn't make you win races."

I breathe in deeply and let it out slowly. I won every single race this summer while wearing them. I know it's a silly superstition, but it's important to me.

I stand in front of where she sits on the mattress, and put my hands on either side of her legs. "I love you."

"I love you," she says back just before I kiss her.

"See you at the races?"

She nods. "See you at the races."

CHAPTER THREE

Keanna

Our hotel room is really nice. The bed is plush and pillow soft, the sheets made of some high thread count. They even smell like fancy laundry detergent. I stayed in a few hotels with Jett this summer, and they all made me feel the same way, like I was wrapped in luxury. These aren't even five-star hotels or anything, they're just nice and clean.

The bathroom has marble countertops and there's a large flat screen TV on the wall, which I turn on to a movie channel. All of this luxury is fun, but it reminds me of my old life, where I had a mom who would make us sleep in the car when we couldn't afford rent. Cheap motel rooms for the night were a luxury and they were already inhabited by the roaches and mice who lived there full time. I used to long for a shower, not even caring how filthy the motel was, just because I hadn't showered in days.

I'm glad I didn't know about these nice hotels back then. I don't think I could have handled it.

I order a strawberry banana smoothie from room service and lay back in bed and enjoy the peaceful serenity of our room with a balcony that overlooks the city of San Antonio, which isn't like Houston at all. It's sprawling, with shorter buildings, and not much of a big downtown area. The land is hilly and sloping, unlike the flatness of Houston. It's pretty here, in its own way. It's not as busy and filled with people or traffic.

When it's almost time for the heat races to start, I push myself up out of the super plush mattress. It's a chore leaving a bed that comfortable, but I'm excited to watch Jett race.

I stand up, and step right on top of my suitcase which I'd left next to the bed. I jump, afraid to put much weight on it because my laptop is in there.

That's when I squeeze the Styrofoam smoothie cup too hard, and the last few inches of strawberry banana spill out all over the place.

Ugh.

I rush into the bathroom and clean off, but my shorts are pretty much ruined for the day. I kick them off, toss them over the edge of the bathtub and then get a new pair. Luckily, it all went down my legs and missed my shirt, so I leave that on.

I grab my phone and my room key and head down to the lobby. Outside, the stadium looms in the distance. It looks so small compared to the large arenas we've been to in other states. I don't even know if they could host a football game in this one.

I walk toward it, slipping into line with the rest of the spectators. I know I have a pit pass to visit Jett after he races, but for the actual race, I want to sit in the stands so I get a good view. My name is on the will-call list, so they let me in and I make my way down to the section of seats in front of the finish line, which is always the best place to watch a dirt bike race.

The place is buzzing with excited spectators. Children wearing T-shirts of their favorite racer, and parents doing the same. Some little kids play in the aisle next to me with toy dirt bikes. They make the motor sound and have the bikes jump in the air and then tumble downward. I don't know why they like making the bikes crash so much. In real life, that's the worst thing to happen in a race.

The smell of exhaust fills the air as the first heat race lines up at the gate. I scan the number plates of all the bikes, but Jett isn't in this one, so I'm only half paying attention.

I see what Jett meant about the arenacross tracks being different—they're tiny! There's a ton of jumps and turns but it's all jam packed together, and even the track itself is only wide enough for maybe four bikes at a time. At home, our motocross track is huge and it fills several acres. There's hills and long jumps and little jumps and big sweeping turns, with three long straight ways. You can enjoy yourself on a track like ours at home, but here it's all business.

A woman wearing lots of perfume slides across the aisle and sits two seats down from me. She's also wearing a lot of hairspray in her poufy hair, and she reminds me of Dolly Parton. She's as Texas as it gets and it makes me smile.

"Darlin, you here alone?" she asks me after a few minutes of watching the races. She has one heavily painted one eyebrow lifted in concern.

I nod. "Kind of."

She lifts the other eyebrow.

"My boyfriend is racing," I explain, nodding toward the track. "So I'm here with him, but I'm sitting alone."

She takes her Diet Coke bottle from the cup holder

in her chair and moves over to sit next to me. "Not anymore, you're not," she says with a grin. "My son is out there, number fifteen."

She points to the starting line and I find him on a Honda. He's wearing a lime green helmet that clashes with his otherwise read and black riding gear.

"Nice helmet," I say.

She nods. "I make him wear it so I can see him out there," she says with a grin. "It's so hard to tell one kid from another when they're going so fast!"

I don't tell her that it's pretty easy for me to spot Jett because he's always up at the front. I just nod. "That's a pretty good idea."

"Moms know best," she says. "My name is Marisol, by the way."

"I'm Keanna," I say.

She cocks her head. "Keanna? I've only heard that name once. You're not that famous boy's girlfriend, are you?" Her eyes go wide. "What's his name...he's the son of Jace Adams."

"Jett," I say.

"No way!" she says. "Are you her?"

"That's me..." It feels so awkward being asked this question by a grown woman. Usually, on the very rare times that I've been recognized, it's been a teenage girl asking me.

She squeezes my arm and beams at me. "That is so amazing! My son is going to be so mad that I got to meet you and he didn't."

I feel my cheeks go warm. "Why would he care to meet me?"

She laughs, and glances out at the track to keep an eye on her son. He's back in the middle of the racers, probably tenth place or so. "Well, honey, he'd say it's because he's a big fan of Jett, but I think he has a crush on you." She winks at me and then gazes back out at the track. "We saw you and Jace's wife once at that track out in Lawson, Texas and he went all googly eyed and wanted to go say hi to you. Never got the guts though." She looks over at me, grinning through her long fake eyelashes. "Of course, I told him he ain't got a chance in hell when you're dating Jett." She winks at me. "Girl, I had the biggest crush on his daddy when I was young. That's about the only reason I went with my dad and brother to all their motocross races. I was hoping to see Jace."

I laugh. "Yeah, I've heard stories like that."

Jett's dad is definitely cute in an older guy way, and I know Bayleigh had to put up with girls throwing themselves at him all the time. Now I'm in the same position with Jett, but I never thought a guy would like *me*. It's kind of flattering.

We finish watching the race, and Marisol's son takes ninth place which is just good enough to guarantee him a spot in the real races tomorrow. She tells me about how he's a private racer and has been hoping to get some sponsorships but they haven't happened yet. They live in Dallas, right in the heart of the city, so he didn't get to grow up riding every day like some of the other guys did.

After two more heat races, it's finally time for Jett to qualify. I watch him ride out to the starting line. Marcus and Clay walk up behind him, and talk with him before the races. Now I kind of wished I would have used my VIP pass to go down there and tell him good luck before the race. But there's not enough time to go down to the pits and then come back up here to get a good view, and I love watching him ride.

"You can tell your boy knows what he's doing," Marisol says as Jett lines up at the starting gate and pulls his goggles over his helmet. "He's got that confident posture. He's a pro already. My boy needs to learn more of that."

"Jett had a good teacher," I say with a smile. It may seem silly, but it's a total turn on when I see Jett on the track, especially compared to other guys. He's a pro. He's good at what he does, and it shows. He never bumbles along the track or looks foolish. He is sleek and skilled and fast as hell. My chest fills with pride as I watch him.

The racers rev their engines and wait for the gate to drop. As it falls, Jett takes off, pulling the lead just like I knew he would.

Marisol squees in delight as we watch him go, pulling a bigger lead every second. Today's race will be easy because he's riding with people who are trying to qualify. Tomorrow, when he's riding with all of the best racers, it'll be more of a challenge. Today though, he almost seems bored. Before long, Jett's got such a huge lead that he's coming up on the racers who are in last place. He passes a few of them, meaning he's over a whole lap ahead of those guys, and I lose sight of the guy in second place as he gets caught up racing around the guys in last place.

Jett is easy to spot though, not because he has a crazy colored helmet or anything, but because of his style on the track. The way he carries himself, the way he throws his whole body along with the bike over the jumps and then ducks down low to sweep through a sharp turn. I'd recognize his racing style anywhere.

He comes up on a section of whoops, which are tiny jumps that are so close together you can't exactly jump them. It's like gliding your bike over a bunch of speed bumps in a parking lot, only they're about three feet tall.

Everything seems to go in slow motion as I watch one of the straggling racers in front of Jett wobble on the whoops. His handlebars yank sideways and then his whole bike flops and he's thrown to the ground. Normally I wouldn't think twice, only he does this right in front of my boyfriend.

Jett's bike is going too fast to slow down or get out of the way. His front tire crashes into the side of the guy's bike and Jett flies forward, tumbling over the wreckage. I jump straight out of my seat as his body seems to float in the air for a second and then he crashes face first into the next jump, his leg bent around behind him.

"Shit!" I stand here, fists clenched at my side, waiting for him to jump up and run back to his bike. He's got a big enough lead that he still has plenty of time to get back on the track and keep his first place lead. But he doesn't get up right away.

One of the guys on the track rushes over and waves a yellow flag, which signals to the other racers that they need to slow down because they're approaching a crash scene.

The first guy who fell in front of Jett gets up and dusts himself off, then goes to pull his bike away from Jett's.

I stare at Jett's helmeted head, watching as he wobbles and tries to climb to his feet, but he's not moving very fast. He must have been dazed. Marcus runs across the track, rushing to his aid, and another track guy picks up Jett's bike and rolls it over to him. Now all Jett has to do is get up and get back on it and start racing again. He's taking so long, and each second that passes is going to be harder for him to secure first place.

But first place doesn't matter right now, I tell myself. He needs to place in the top ten to move on to tomorrow's race. This will be fine.

The track guy tries to give Jett his bike back, but Marcus shakes his head. What? What the hell does that mean?

He's kneeling down beside Jett, who is moving, but barely. I see the paramedics on a golf cart speed down the side of the arena, heading toward Jett.

"Oh shit," Marisol says beside me. "He might be hurt."

I turn to her, eyes wide, because she just said exactly what I've been afraid to admit to myself.

I run down the stadium aisle and toward the VIP area, barely missing crashing into popcorn vendors in my haste. I get to the blue doors that say EMPLOYEE'S ONLY and there's two big muscled guys wearing polo shirts with the stadium's logo on it. They block my way. "You need a VIP pass to get in here," one of them says.

"I've got one!" I say, shoving my hand in my back

pocket. But all I feel is my cell phone. Panic courses through me as I check my other pocket, and then all of them again. Where the hell is it?

Of course. The shorts I left in the bathroom of the hotel. They had the pass in it. I curse under my breath and look up at the guys, trying to seem innocent. "Is there any way you can let me in? Please? My boyfriend is racing and he just got hurt."

They both shake their head.

I turn around and walk as quickly as I can to the doors that lead outside. And then I run.

The stadium is round, and a third of the way down is where the entrance is for the racers. They're all parked outside in the parking lot, but they have to get inside the stadium somehow, and this is how I'll do it, too.

There are people all over the place, managers like Marcus, and other dirt bike people who put on the races. I keep my head up and I pretend that I'm totally supposed to be here and hope no one says anything.

There's an ambulance parked back here, and right when I walk past it, two EMTs run up and climb inside. They drive the ambulance forward to the doors that lead to the stadium, and then the back door opens and a female EMT jumps out, lowering a stretcher. I see the two guys from the golf cart pull up, and they're carrying

Jett on one of those orange plastic stretcher things. My heart skips a beat and I run toward him.

"Stay back," one of the EMTs says, holding out a hand to stop me.

My heart is racing as I try to catch a glimpse of him, but he's got an oxygen mask on his face, and he seems really out of it. They load him into the ambulance, and I rush forward. "Please," I say to whoever will listen. "I need to go with him!"

"Family only," the woman says, not even looking at me in her haste to get Jett into the ambulance.

It feels a little gross, but I say what I need to say. "I'm his sister!"

She looks back at me, lifting an eyebrow as she gives me a once over. "Please!" I say. "I'm the only family member here with him."

"Get on in," she says.

CHAPTER
FOUR

Jett

When I open my eyes, it's bright as hell in here. My head is killing me, but it feels slow as well. Sluggish. This isn't the first time I've woken up in a cold hospital room with all the sense knocked out of me. I get it immediately. I know why I'm here.

Dirt bikes. It has to be.

I close my eyes and try to focus on my breathing, hoping my rapid heartbeat will calm down if only to make that stupid machine shut up. Where the hell am I and what race is it?

That's right. Details come back to me slowly. San Antonio. Heat race.

I couldn't get out of the way fast enough.

"Shit," I say, opening my eyes. I get a bright dose of hospital lights and I lift my head, but I can't sit up much. I'm groggy, heavily drugged from the feel of it.

"Hello!" I call out. There's hospital blankets on top of me, and I smell like sweat. I look down and see my leg is in a cast. Fuck.

A cast. A real one, plaster and all, not just a walking cast or a splint.

This is not good.

A curtain opens and a white coat doctor with graying hair appears with a cheerful smile on his face. I look around find myself surrounded in these white curtain walls. That explains why it's so damn loud in here. We must be in the ER.

"Hello, Mr. Adams," the doctor says in a booming voice.

"Mr. Adams is my dad," I say on impulse, although that doesn't really matter right now.

"How's your head feeling?" the doctor asks.

"Like shit. What's wrong with me? My leg? Anything else? How bad is it?"

I try sitting up on my elbows but I quickly fall back down because the drugs are making me woozy. The doctor chuckles. "Just take it easy, son. You're not in too bad of shape. Just a minor concussion and a fractured tibia."

I sigh and curse under my breath. "A fracture is a big deal, doc."

"You'll be healed up in about six weeks," he says, giving me an assuring smile that does absolutely nothing to assure me.

"Six weeks is a lifetime in my world."

He chuckles again and holds a narrow flashlight up to my eyes. He does a few more checks and says some more shit about how I'll be able to leave the hospital today and that my head isn't that bad. I don't pay much attention. All I'm thinking about how is how I can't race for Team Loco for the next six freaking weeks. This might ruin me. What if Marcus kicks me off the team?

The tail end of something the doctor says catches my attention. "Your sister is here, so she'll be in here soon..."

I look at him. "My sister?"

He nods. "She's here. You do have a sister, right? I'm tired of these dirt bike guys being followed around by stalkers claiming to be family members."

I nod slowly. "I have a sister but—my parents are here?"

"No, just your sister. She told me you live few hours away."

That doesn't make any sense. My sister is a baby. How the hell is she here?

The doctor opens the curtain and motions to someone, and then Keanna appears. She's got a timid smile as she slips past the doctor and approaches my bed.

"Hey," she says. "Good thing I was here because they only let *family* join you." She gives me wink.

I grin. "Thanks, sis."

The doctor tells us someone will be in here shortly to discharge me and then we're left alone.

"Oh my God, Jett," Keanna whispers. She grabs my hand and squeezes it. "You scared the hell out of me." Tears immediately flood her eyes and roll down her cheeks. I reach up and swipe them off, cupping her face in my hand.

"Baby, I'm okay."

She shakes her head, blinking quickly to clear the tears. "You're not okay. You have a broken leg and a concussion. I watched you crash and you didn't get up and it was the worst thing ever."

She takes a ragged breath. "It's just—I'm just glad you're okay."

Seeing her makes me happy, and for about thirty seconds I feel relieved and glad to be with her. Then it all comes back to me, the reality of my situation and how

I've just been injured on the first damn race of the season.

"This sucks," I say, covering my eyes with the hand that's not holding onto Keanna. "I'm out for six weeks."

"Marcus is waiting in the lobby," she says. "He's not mad," she adds after my eyes go wide. "He's just really concerned about you. He sent Clay in to race after you left, and he qualified in the next heat race so Team Loco is still being represented tomorrow."

I nod slowly. "That's good."

She squeezes my hand. "Marcus wants you to focus on getting better and then he's putting you right back into the races. He told me to tell you that so you wouldn't be mad."

I chuckle. "So, he's not kicking me off the team."

"No way." She leans down and kisses me. "You're just on a short hiatus."

"Hey now," I say, giving her a playful look. "Sisters don't kiss their brothers like that."

She turns beet red. "Shut up! I had to say it so they'd let me on the ambulance."

I run my thumb across her palm, staring at the ring I gave her. "We should get married. Then you'll have all legal rights to be with my broken ass in the hospital."

She swallows. "What, like right now?"

I shrug. "I don't know. Soon. I mean...that's where we're headed, right?"

Her lips break into a smile that's so sweet it makes my heart hurt. "I hope so," she says quietly. "But you can't just marry me because it makes it easier to get into your hospital room."

"That's not why I'd be marrying you," I say. It's a sweet moment, but a nurse interrupts us by barging in and talking about the discharge procedure. I'm loaded into a wheelchair and rolled outside where Marcus is waiting in my truck to take me back to my hotel.

Every freaking bump on the road sends pain shooting through my head, but I believe the doctor when he says my concussion isn't too bad. I've had worse. My leg aches as well, so the hospital meds are probably starting to wear off.

Clay and Marcus help me get into a wheelchair the hotel has on hand while Keanna looks at me like I'm go into break into pieces if I'm not handled carefully. "I'm fine," I tell her. "I'll be able to walk on crutches after my freaking head gets a little better."

"We're getting you a wheelchair," she says, her face resolute. "I have to go fill your pain med prescription so I'll get a wheelchair, too."

"I'll drive you," Clay tells her as we all pile into the hotel elevator.

"Thank you," she says, giving him a smile. She puts a hand on my shoulder. "You're going straight to bed, mister. No walking around. You need to rest."

"Shit, how the hell am I going to get us home tomorrow?" I say, looking down at my foot. I can't exactly drive with a huge ass cast on my right foot.

"I'll drive us," she says. Despite how she's scared of big trucks and she's never driven mine at all, she says it with confidence and a tone in her voice that says I'm not allowed to argue.

I kind of like it when she gets like this. It's totally sexy.

When I'm in my hotel room, Clay and Keanna head to the nearest pharmacy and my heart immediately beats a little harder in what is most definitely jealousy. I'm glad it's Clay with her though...the other guys on my team would no doubt try to hit on her. But Clay only cares about motocross, so hitting on my girlfriend would be the last thing on his mind.

Marcus gets me a soda and hangs around while we wait for them to get back. I know the procedure—get a concussion, have everyone watch you like a baby for a few hours. It's annoying.

"You got a good girlfriend," Marcus says.

"Trust me, I know."

He laughs. "I've seen so many motocross fangirls in

my life, and they're always in it for the wrong reasons. Not that girl, though."

"I know what you mean." I pile the pillows on the bed so I can sit up on them. "She's the best."

"When I was racing, I never had a steady girlfriend," Marcus says. "They were all in it for the wrong damn reasons."

Marcus was a pro racer about twenty years ago, but he only lasted three years before his parents died in a car wreck and he quit to take care of his siblings. My dad knew him a little bit, but Marcus was older than him so they never raced together.

I'm pretty sure he's been single his whole life, or at least never married. You never see Marcus with a girl-friend, and he never talks about dating anybody, but maybe he just keeps that part of his life to himself.

"I'm going to marry her," I say.

Marcus holds out his can of soda to me in a toast. "I bet you will, Adams. I want to be invited to the wedding."

I grin. "You better get us a badass wedding gift."

CHAPTER
FIVE

Keanna

I DON'T KNOW MUCH about Clay, so it's a little weird walking with him to the nearby pharmacy. He's tall, taller than Jett, and a little wider too. Tattoos line both of his arms, some of them colorful and some are just black shadows and shapes. I find myself trying to sneak a glimpse of them without being too obvious.

He used to have hair, which he kept floppy and in need of a haircut. That's how he looked when I first saw him on the Team Loco website. But a few months ago, he shaved it all off and now he looks like a scary bouncer at a nightclub.

"You gotta make me a promise, okay?" Clay asks me as we walk.

"Um...okay?" We barely know each other so it feels weird that he wants promises from me.

He gives me a hesitant smile. "Now that Jett's out of the season for a few weeks, Marcus is going to put me in the races in his spot. There's no denying that Jett is the faster guy here, that's why I got second place and he got first in the summer series. I just—" He runs his hand across his head, almost as if he expected to be able to run his fingers through his hair. He sighs, letting the air out slowly through his lips.

"I'm not trying to upstage him or anything, okay?"

"No one thinks you are," I say. This is a new side of Clay, the timid and slightly worried side. He's always seemed too uptight and serious when I've been around him.

He nods quickly but he still looks nervous. "I don't want Jett to be pissed at me for taking over, you know? If you could just, I don't know, like say nice things about me to him? Let him know I feel like shit and I hate that he got injured."

"I think he knows that, Clay. It's not like you jumped out and pushed him off his bike or anything."

He shrugs. "This is a competitive field. I can already see the articles now...journalists asking me if I'm happy I got another chance to up my race stats and take over as the top rookie..." He shakes his head. "Jett and I are teammates. I want it to stay that way. I'm on his side."

"I'll make sure he knows," I promise.

At the pharmacy, Clay opens the door for me. While I get Jett's prescriptions filled, Clay walks around the store, collecting random items. We make our way to the front desk to pay, and Clay dumps it all on the counter.

"It's on me," he tells me, taking out his wallet.

"What is it?" I say, lifting an eyebrow at the stuff he's chosen.

"A care package for Jett. Magazines I know he loves, candy, junk food, a phone charger because he was complaining that he left his at home, and some Band-Aids."

"Band-Aids?" I ask.

Clay smirks, handing his credit card to the cashier. "Inside joke."

Clay holds the bags of stuff as we make our way the three blocks to the hotel. "Don't take this the wrong way," I begin.

"Uh oh," Clay says. "Those words are almost always followed by something I'll take the wrong way."

I laugh. "It's just that you're actually a cool guy."

He grins. "That wasn't so bad."

I scratch my arm and glance over at his tattoos again.

"You just seem like a boulder. Like this mean asshole who doesn't ever know how to smile."

"Okay, that was mean," he says sarcastically.

"I told you not to take it the wrong way!" I say, slapping him on the arm.

He chuckles. "It's cool. I get that a lot. I'm just a quiet guy most of the time. I don't care for small talk or any of that shit, unless I'm with friends."

"So are we friends?" I ask.

He throws an arm around my shoulder. "Looks like we are."

The next morning, I pack up all of our stuff even though Jett wants to help. I have to glare at him and tell him to keep his ass in the bed where he belongs. The last thing he needs is to break his other leg while hobbling around the hotel room packing a suitcase.

"Baby..." Jett says in a whining voice. "I'm not an invalid. Let me help."

"You're recovering from a concussion," I say, giving him a pointed stare. "Your butt stays on that bed until I say so."

"You're even worse than my mom," he says.

I heft the suitcase onto the bed and zip it closed. "What'd she say about all of this?"

He snorts. "She hasn't said a damn thing because I haven't told her."

I put my hands on my hips. "You were in the hospital with a concussion and a broken leg and you didn't call your mom?"

He shrugs. "Why should I?"

"Because she cares about you!"

"It's not that bad of an injury," he says, but he does look a little guilty. "I would have called her if it was something bad."

I roll my eyes. "Give me your phone."

His eyes widen and he grabs the phone off the nightstand, pressing it against his chest. "She's just going to worry."

"No, she's going to be pissed that you didn't call and tell her immediately."

Jett sighs and holds out his phone. "You're right."

I take it and call Bayleigh. I was right, of course. She was not thrilled to hear about Jett's injury a day after it happened. But she tells us to be careful getting home and even offers to drive up to get us. I tell her we're fine, and that leads me to the obstacle I've been avoiding.

Driving Jett's truck.

It's huge, with an extended cab and big tires and it

feels like a monster on the road, especially compared to my tiny Mustang back home. It's small and close to the road and I feel comfortable in my own car. I haven't been driving long and Jett's truck feels like a monster I'd have to wrangle into submission. But I'm doing this for him, and for me, to prove we can handle anything.

Jett climbs into his truck just fine by himself, even though I stand around to make sure.

"Baby, it's a broken leg. I'm fine, really," he says, kissing me just before I close the passenger door for him.

My heart pounds as I walk over to the driver's side, the part of this truck I've only ever been near when I'm kissing Jett goodbye from the outside. With a deep breath, I grab the handle and yank open the door, then I climb inside as if I'm totally cool with this.

After all, I do know how to drive. It's a straight shot back to Lawson, just a few hours of interstate and then we'll be home. I can do this.

"You look sexy in a truck," Jett says, winking at me as I start the engine.

"You look sexier than I do in the driver's seat," I say.

He grabs my leg and squeezes it, then reaches up and brushes my hair behind my ear. "Baby, you're a great driver. Don't let the truck intimidate you. You've got this."

My heart warms and I return his smile. Then I put the truck in gear and pull out of the parking lot.

I was right about the interstate. It's not so bad driving on it because there are no turns or red lights. By the time we get back to Lawson, Jett's pain meds have kicked in and he's asleep in the passenger seat. I feel a sense of pride at being the girlfriend who can handle things when he's injured. It feels empowering, too. Like we're both partners here.

When we get home, Jett's dad meets us in the driveway with a pair of crutches that are covered in dirt bike stickers. Jett laughs when he sees them.

"They're lucky crutches," Jace explains to me when I give them both a weird look. "They've got me through a few broken bones and Jett's used them twice."

"Good ol' Crutchy," Jett says, winking at me. "I named them when I was five and Dad had broken his ankle. I wasn't very creative."

I roll my eyes and open the truck's back door to retrieve our luggage, but Jace stops me. "I'll get this stuff, hon."

"Thanks," I tell him, then I rush ahead to open the back door for Jett.

"You're the best," Jett tells me as he crutches on by me and into the house. He leans forward and gives me a kiss, then hobbles into the kitchen. I can hear Brooke crying from another room, which is probably where Bayleigh is.

Upstairs, Jett settles onto his futon, with snacks and drinks next to him and a video game loaded into the Xbox.

"I think you're all set," I say, surveying the scene I've put together.

Jett leans his head back on the futon and gives me a sultry look. "I'm missing one girlfriend," he says, patting his lap. "Come here."

We make out a little bit, but I cut it short because tomorrow is Monday and my first college classes start. I scoot off his lap and sit on the futon next to him, keeping my arm wrapped around his shoulder.

"I love you, but I need to go."

He frowns, jutting out his bottom lip. "But I've heard that kissing makes bones heal faster."

"I'd love to see the scientific evidence on that," I say.

He grins and slides a hand up my leg, his fingers sliding under the hem of my shorts. "Let's do our own research."

My stomach flutters. I pull him closer and kiss him, parting my lips and letting his tongue do some exploring. His touch sends a fire up my belly, and before I know it,

I'm allowing myself to be pulled onto his lap once again, my body grinding against his, his hands feeling up my shirt. I grab his hair and lightly tug his head back, breaking our kiss.

"I have to go," I say, grinning at him.

"I know," he says. He grabs my butt and rocks me against him. "You're free to leave whenever you want."

I close my eyes and take a deep breath. It's after ten at night and I have school at nine in the morning. "I love you," I say just before I climb off him and try to gain my composure.

"Love you more," he says back, giving me a wink.

Downstairs, Bayleigh stops me before I leave.

"What's up?" I say, trying to look cool and not like I just made out with her son.

She shifts Brooke onto her hip and gives me a sad smile. "Just wanted to give you a little warning about Jett. He's just like his dad," she says, rolling her eyes in this sarcastic way. "When he gets hurt, he's going to be pissed that he can't ride, and it might feel like he's mad at you. But he's not, okay?"

My brows pull together. "He seemed okay just now."

"That's good," she says. "But six weeks is a long time. If he starts becoming an asshole, just know it's not you that he's mad at. He's mad at himself, okay? Don't be afraid to put him in his place if he starts being an ass."

I smile. "I'll keep that in mind."

"Good," she says, patting my arm. "Have a good night. And good luck at school tomorrow!"

CHAPTER
SIX

Jett

THE WEIRD THING about a broken leg is that it doesn't hurt so much after a couple of weeks. My arms hurt more than anything because they're sick of using the crutches, but my foot feels okay. Too bad I can't actually walk on it yet. I have four more weeks before I can get a walking cast and even then, the doctor doesn't want me riding a bike just yet.

This whole situation sucks balls.

Keanna's taking college classes, so to fill the void, I've been doing her job at The Track almost every single day.

All I have to do is sit behind the counter and deal with customers, and it's boring as shit, but at least I feel useful. The worst part is when my friends come in to ride and I know they'll be having a blast on the track while I'm stuck here, immobile and wasting away.

I hit the gym in the evenings, working on arms, chest, and back so I can stay at least a little bit in shape. I do everything I can to stay busy, but it doesn't help much.

By October, I'm fighting a losing battle with depression. All I want to do is hit the track. Feel the bike underneath me, the motor roaring in my ears. I want to travel again and revel in the feel of being the first racer to fly over the finish line jump. But now Clay gets that privilege and I'm stuck at home.

The boredom is driving me crazy. I don't know how Keanna handles working at The Track so much. Just a couple of weeks being stuck behind this counter drives me crazy. I don't want to be inside, I want to be outside, on the track.

It is nice that I get to see my girlfriend more often, but she's stressed with midterms and college essays and reading assignments, so she's kind of in her own world.

On a particularly cold October day, every one must decide to stay home because I'm stuck sitting here in the front office for three hours without seeing a single person. My mom is at home with Brooke, and Dad is giving a lesson. I'm not sure where Keanna's parents are, but she's in class right now, a three hour lecture on history.

I doodle on a notebook until I run out of paper and then I look around the office for something else to distract me. But there is nothing, and that heavy weight of depression that's been lurking around the corner is closer than ever.

I can't ride and that pisses me off.

I'm bored, and that pisses me off.

My leg isn't healed yet, and that also pisses me off.

But none of these things are what's causing the depression. I think it finally hit me, something I guess I've known my whole life but always chose to ignore. This...this boring empty day is exactly what my life would be if I didn't have motocross.

While Keanna is getting an education and making something of herself, I've got nothing. What would happen if I suddenly wasn't able to ride anymore? If I got fired, or injured too badly? I'd become a huge burden on my family. Keanna would have no reason to be with me anymore. She'd have lots of opportunities to meet college guys who are better than me and can give her the life she deserves.

I let these thoughts consume me for the next hour. Anxiety fills my thoughts, followed quickly by anger and depression. Without motocross, I am truly nothing. I can't go off and create my own dirt bike track like my dad did. I have no skills, no talents. Just motocross.

I turn to the work computer and pull up the local college's website. They list all of their academic programs, but nothing really stands out to me. I don't want to study the earth, or do financial accounting, or produce music albums. I don't want to do any of this crap.

A deeper level of panic hits me when I realize that I can't even come up with a backup plan if everything about college doesn't fit me. There's not a single college degree that interests me. Plus, where would I find the time for a fallback education in case motocross doesn't work out?

What the hell have I been thinking all my life?

Only idiots think they can become famous and keep that fame forever. I need money. A career. A backup plan.

I'm so stressed I've developed a migraine. I look under the front desk for some aspirin, but I can't find any. My crutches are next to me, but the thought of hobbling down to the break room sounds like too much effort for my already exhausted brain. I lower my head to the counter and close my eyes, letting the cool stainless steel surface wash over my forehead.

"Babe?" Keanna's voice is soft and tender, just like she is in real life.

My eyes flutter open. I don't know how long I've been asleep, but my migraine is still here, thundering around in my skull. Keanna peers at me, looking overly concerned, just like she's been since the day I got hurt. Her hand touches my back.

"Are you okay?"

I shrug and sit up slowly, the pain in my head rocketing around with the movement. "Just bored."

Her lips press into a thin line. "You look sick."

"My head hurts," I add.

"What about your leg? Do you need some pain meds?"

I nod. "Please."

What I don't ask for is enough alcohol to knock me into a drunken stupor. Being able to forget about all of my flaws sounds like a perfect idea right now.

"Baby, you seem weird," Keanna says a few minutes after watching me down my pain meds. She's sitting on the stool next to me. We can't leave since The Track is technically still open for a few hours, even though no one is here.

I look over at her, a lie balancing on the tip of my

tongue. It'd be easy to tell her that I'm fine. That nothing at all is wrong. But she'd know better.

"Just thinking about life," I mutter, taking another sip of the water she'd brought me.

"Baby..." her hand slides up and down my back. "You'll be back on your bike in no time."

"Yeah, until I get hurt again."

Her hand stops moving. "You don't get hurt very often, Jett. It probably won't happen again."

I shake my head. "You don't know that. It's all chance. But it's worse than chance...chance is that you might get hurt in a car wreck. What I do is choose to ride a dirt bike all the time, and that's a much more dangerous thing than driving." I slam the bottle of water down so hard it makes her jump.

"What I've chosen is a career that will most definitely get me hurt over and over again." I look at her, noticing for the first time that she's wearing the dark purple scarf I'd bought her from my trip to Washington. I swallow. "What happens when I don't recover in a few weeks? What happens when I fuck up my knee or my wrist or my head, and I can't ride anymore?"

Her gaze darkens. "Baby...you're just thinking about the worst right now. It's going to be okay."

I shake my head and stare out the window in front of us, looking out at the empty fields across the road.

"Underneath this motocross thing, I'm a nobody. A total loser."

"You are not," she says, standing off her stool. "You're an amazing person. So what that your leg is broken? You'll heal and you'll be fine."

I shrug. "I just can't stop thinking about how one day I might not recover fully and I'll be off the team. One day will come where I can't race motocross anymore. What will I do then? You'll have a fancy degree and a good job and I'll be stuck being the idiot loser that you have to take care of."

She laughs. It's a little chuckle at first, but then she bursts into pure, unfiltered laughter. "Oh my God, Jett..." she puts a hand to her chest and forces herself to stop laughing.

I sit up straighter and cross my arms over my chest while I wait for her to stop laughing.

"You think I've got this shit figured out? I have no idea what I'm doing, either. Nobody does. I don't even think most adults know what they're doing."

I frown. "How are you so cool with this? I'm potentially a big failure with no career prospects to fall back on.

She shakes her head. "That's not true. You have this place, The Track. You have experience and skills and fame. You could become a reporter on motocross, or a race announcer, or the manager of a team like Marcus. You could do all kinds of things." She reaches for my hand. "Besides, baby. You still have a lot of racing ahead of you."

"What if I don't?" I say softly, as I stare at her hand in mine. "What if the next crash is what does me in? Stops me from racing forever?"

She shrugs. "What if a meteor crashes through the roof in three seconds and kills us both?"

Everything is quiet for a few seconds. I look up at the ceiling, then exhale. "Glad that didn't happen."

She punches me in the arm. "See? Everything is fine."

I reach out and run my fingers down her chin, taking in how purely beautiful she is and how she has the ability to be calm and serious when I'm freaking out. I breathe in deeply and then pull her toward me for a kiss.

"Sorry I freaked on you, baby doll," I whisper against her lips. "I'm just not having a good day."

"Not every day is a good one," she says, pressing her forehead to mine. "But no matter what, I'll always be here with you. Sink or swim, win or lose."

I grin, and some of my fear washes away beneath the power of her loving gaze. I wrap my arms around her and tug her toward me. She gets off her stool and positions herself between my legs, her hands finding their way around my chest.

"We're soul mates," she says. "Where you go, I go."

"What if where I go is Loserville?"

She shrugs. "It doesn't matter where we are. As long as we're together."

CHAPTER
SEVEN

Keanna

I CAN'T BELIEVE I thought my college history class would be easy. This is all the internet's fault. My instructor, Mr. Garrett, has high ratings on ratemyprofessor.com, and everyone says he's a super easy teacher and it's not hard at all to get an A. That's the exact reason I chose his class when I signed up.

Now that I'm a few weeks into the semester, I should leave a bad review on all of those former students because they are totally wrong. Mr. Garrett is nice enough, but his entire curriculum involves listening to him lecture on various unrelated history stories and then taking a test over a million vocabulary words. I spent the first couple of weeks of class wasting my time taking notes on his lectures. They literally don't matter at all. I think he just likes to lecture to hear himself talk.

At the end of the week, he gives us a ten page (or longer) print out of just history vocabulary words, and that's what the test is based on. And then the text is the very next day. I wish he would give us the vocab words at the start of the week, so I could spend my hours in class studying instead of listening to him go on and on about history.

I adjust positions on my bed. My legs and back ache from sitting up so long hunched over my study sheet. I straighten my legs and stretch my arms over my head.

There's a soft knock on my door.

"Come in," I call out.

The door opens, and I look over.

And scream.

Jett bursts into laughter and pulls up the hideous Halloween monster mask, revealing his normal face underneath. "Oh my God, I got you," he says, leaving the mask on top of his hair while he crutches himself into my room.

My heart is still racing from the split second of total fear, and I put a hand to my chest, taking a deep breath. "I will get you back," I say.

He winks. "I'd love to see you try."

The bed sinks when he sits down next to me. He pulls off the mask and tosses it to the floor, then leans his crutches against my dresser.

"Still studying?"

"Yeah," I say with a groan. "I'm sick of it, but I only know about half of these terms so far."

Jett takes my vocabulary list and looks it over. "When's your test?"

"Tomorrow."

"What? What kind of asshole gives a test on Halloween?"

I chuckle. "College classes don't care what day it is."

"That's crap," he says, frowning. He slides over to the foot of my bed and holds the list in front of him. "Do you want me to ask you the word or the definition?"

"You don't have to study with me, babe." I reach for the papers back, but he holds them out of my reach. "I'm serious. It's super boring."

He shrugs. "I'd rather be bored with you than bored without you."

It's a simple sentence, but it makes me blush a little. I love that he can still do this to me, make me feel special and wanted even after all these months of dating.

I lean back against my headboard and let him ask me the questions. We study until I've got them all memorized, at least enough that I'll be able to choose the definition off Mr. Garrett's multiple choice test.

After our study session, I make some popcorn and bring it back up to my room, and Jett turns on Netflix. He leans his back against my headboard, his broken foot out in front of him like a large rock at the foot of my bed. I lean against his chest, my feet curled up underneath me. I love the way his arm holds onto my shoulders, and how every time I lean against him, it's like his arm is magnetized to hold onto me. He never forgets that I'm right here next to him.

"So my mom told me we're on candy duty tomorrow," Jett says.

"Try not to eat it all like you did last time," I say, elbowing him in the stomach. He laughs.

"Do you think I can wear this mask?" He pulls it back over his head. It's some kind of hairy monster with a snarling mouth. "Or will it be too scary for the little kids?" His voice is muffled from the mask.

I tilt my head. "You'll be fine. I mean, it's not much different from how your normal face looks."

"Oh, I'm going to get you for that one," Jett says. He dives on top of me and begins tickling my sides. I squeal and fall back on my bed, struggling to get him off me. His creepy monster mask hovers over my face.

"I love you."

I shake my head. "I'm afraid I can't love a grotesque monster like you."

He lifts up the mask, and his normal gorgeous face smiles down at me. "What about now?"

My lips slide to the side of my mouth and I take a long time, like I'm thinking it over. "I guess," I say with a sly grin. "But I mean, I'm not seeing much difference from when you had the mask on."

He kisses me. "Better sleep with one eye open, sweetheart. Me and this mask have a lot of scaring to do."

He winks at me and I roll my eyes. "I can't believe it's already Halloween. Seems like this year just started."

"Are you saying time flies when you're spending it with me?" he asks with that cocky grin of his.

I grab his shoulders and pull him down for a kiss. "Something like that."

Since it's Halloween, the Track stays open a few hours later for a fun party. We turn on the track lights and let people ride, and Bayleigh and my mom decorate the main building in spooky Halloween decorations. Creepy music plays through the track's speakers, and Jett and I sit on the bleachers, handing out candy to trick-ortreaters and the occasional person stopping by on a dirt bike.

Jett wears his scary mask, but I'm dressed up like Tina Belcher from my favorite TV show, Bob's Burgers. A lot of people immediately recognize me, which is fun.

After a group of kids leaves, Jett turns to me, his scary monster face blocking him from my view.

"Your birthday is coming up," he says.

I lift an eyebrow. "Wow, I forgot about that." My nineteenth birthday is in three days. Funny how it hasn't even crossed my mind lately.

"I haven't forgotten." Jett says. His head drops and I imagine he's staring at his feet even though I can't tell for sure because of his monster mask. "I had these awesome plans for it, but now that I can't walk much, they're ruined."

"We don't need to do anything fancy. I'm not really into celebrating my birthday anyway."

The monster turns to face me. "But it was going to be so much fun," he says, sounding all disappointed. "An hour away, there's the annual county fair. It's huge, and there's carnival rides and games and a concert every night. I was going to get us horse rides and cotton candy and wristbands that let us ride every ride as much as we want." He looks back down at the bowl of Halloween candy in his lap. "It was going to be the greatest night ever and now there's no way I can hobble on crutches at the fairgrounds. I wouldn't even be able to get into half of the rides, or get on a horse." He heaves a sigh.

I put my hand on his back. "Baby, it's fine. We'll go next year. I'm serious though—I have no plans to celebrate my birthday. It's not a big deal at all."

"I just want to do something special," he says, his voice muffled. "You may not care about your birthday, but I do. You're my favorite person in the world and if you weren't born, my life would suck. So I definitely want to do something, even if it's just low key."

"Let's definitely stay low key," I say. Some little kids walk up and bashfully yell trick-or-treat, ending our conversation for now. We pass out candy and Jett gets stuck talking to some kid's dad who is apparently a big fan.

Once they leave, and we're alone again, Jett lifts up his monster mask. "What would you like to do for your birthday? Dinner somewhere nice?"

I curl my lip. "Not really. I don't really want to go anywhere."

He looks disappointed, his bottom lip poking out just a bit. "Sorry," I say. "I just want to stay in. College is kicking my ass and work is hard and the baby drives me insane half the time. I just kind of want to sit in a quiet room and be alone with you. We could watch movies or something."

"What kind of movies would you like?"

I shrug. "Eighties romantic comedies."

He laughs and pulls his mask back down over his face. He leans over and lovingly bumps me in the arm with his shoulder. "Sounds like a plan, baby doll."

CHAPTER
EIGHT

Jett

I use the wall to balance myself as I climb down the stepladder on one foot. It's much harder than it seems, but I can't put any weight on my broken foot at all. I think it's probably healed for the most part, but stepping on it would break the cast and get me in hot water with my doctor, and probably with Keanna.

When I get to the floor, my broken leg bent at the knee, I hop over to my crutches.

"Jett Adams!" My mom's shrill voice scares the shit out of me, making me jump. I lean against the wall as my crutches fall to the floor.

"Jesus, Mom," I say, turning to look at her. She's got a stack of DVDs in one hand and the other is on her hip. Her eyes narrow at me, her lips pressed into a thin line.

"Are you trying to kill yourself?" She looks from me to the step ladder, then to the window which I've covered with a blackout curtain. She heaves a sigh. "Son, I can do this for you."

"I got it," I say. I bend down and pick up my crutches, then I hobble over to her. She runs her hand down the creases in the brand new curtains, probably wishing I had ironed them first.

Not gonna happen. I wouldn't even know where to find the iron.

"I'll do the rest," she says. "You can't use a step ladder with a cast on one of your feet."

"Mom, it's fine," I say, throwing my arm around her shoulders. She's so much shorter than I am, it's kind of funny, even though she's still glaring at me. "My cast comes off soon, so my leg is already healed by now. They always leave it on way too long anyhow."

She snorts. "Right, okay. I forgot you went to medical school and you know more than your doctors." She rolls her eyes. "Just let me handle the rest of these. You can do something less dangerous."

Tomorrow is Keanna's nineteenth birthday. Since

my awesome county fair idea was dead on arrival, thanks to my broken leg, I've taken her movie idea and turned it into something awesome. If all she wants to do is sit at home and watch movies, I can still make it special.

Upstairs in my house, we have a game room, that's basically just a big open room with a pool table and a TV and some leather recliners for watching movies. The TV is mounted to the wall and it's only forty-seven inches big, so It's not nearly big enough for what I want to do.

I'm buying a projector and a screen and Dad is helping me install them. I pick up the DVDs Mom set on the couch and go through them. She was in charge of finding eighties romantic comedies that she thinks Keanna would like, and judging by all the girly images on the covers, I think she probably nailed it. As soon as Dad gets back from Best Buy, we're going to set up the projector screen which will make a ninety inch theater screen on our wall. It's going to be amazing.

I also bought four blackout curtains to replace the existing girly ones with black and white baroque patterns on them that my mom picked out a long time ago. These are solid black and have a reflector type of material on the back and they promise to block out all sunlight.

I've rented a popcorn machine from a local party

rental place, and bought a ton of candy and drinks, which Mom is helping me set up on a table as if it were a concession stand.

The best part? My parents and Keanna's parents will be hanging out at Keanna's house all day tomorrow, that way the little kids won't be loud and mess up our day. As soon as Keanna comes over, we're go into have a dark movie theater and a stack of movies. I can't think of anything more relaxing, and I really hope she'll love it. The best part, is that it doesn't require any walking, so my stupid broken leg won't ruin the evening.

"What will you be having for dinner?" Mom asks after she's hung up the other three curtains. The old ones are draped over her shoulder.

"I was thinking some kind of takeout," I say. "Whatever Keanna wants, and we'll get it delivered."

Mom nods. "I'm baking her that chocolate cake she loves. Should be done soon if you want to come eat the leftover icing."

"You know I do," I say, rubbing my stomach.

She laughs. "Do you like the movies I picked out?"

"Hell if I know," I say, casting a glance back at them. "It's not about me liking them, it's about her liking them."

"I've raised you right," Mom says before she heads back downstairs.

When Dad gets back from the store, we set up the projector screen. He thought my movie projector idea was so badass that he wanted to buy it himself, to add an extra level of awesome to the game room. I had planned on buying the projector since it was my idea, but I don't complain. Dad and I hang it from the ceiling and run the wires through the attic. He has to do that part, since I'm stuck with my leg.

We screw the retracting screen from the ceiling and pull it down to cover the existing TV on the wall. Our new massive movie screen looks amazing.

"We can watch the dirt bike races on this thing," Dad says as we sit back and admire our handiwork. Right now it's just playing the DVD loading screen for The Breakfast Club but it still looks amazing.

He claps me on the back. "I can't wait until you're back out there racing."

"Me too, Dad." I cast a scornful look at my leg. "Me too."

I overheard Becca telling my mom that she was planning a fancy birthday breakfast for Keanna, so I decide to let her have some family time on the morning of her birthday. She texts me asking if I want to come over, but I know I'll have her the rest of the day, and I think it's so important for her to be with the people who love her the way she never had when she was growing up, so I tell her to come to my house when she's done. Sometimes it sickens me when I remember that her own mother dumped her off with strangers and never came back. How could anyone do that to their own child? I can understand it happening when the child is an infant and the parent is too unfit to raise them. That's the only thing that makes sense...giving up a child you can't take care of for the greater good. But Keanna was practically a legal adult by the time her mom left her. They'd already spent a lifetime together. That's just cold and unforgivable.

Mom's beautiful chocolate cake rests on the dining table, on a fancy crystal cake stand. My baby sister is now seven months old, so Mom lets her lick some icing off her finger. She doesn't seem to like it, which was kind of hilarious because Mom's homemade from scratch chocolate icing is literally the best thing in the world.

I help Mom decorate the table, but she quickly shoos me away, saying I'm not good at sprinkling confetti, whatever that means. It's just confetti!

But somehow, Mom's right. The table looks amazing when she's done with it. A silver tablecloth sparkles under the chandelier and pink and purple confetti is sprinkled perfectly down the center of the table. My parents' presents for Keanna are wrapped much nicer than how I wrapped mine, and they're sitting next to the cake.

Keanna comes over around eleven, once her family breakfast is done. I meet her at the back door with a kiss and a birthday hug. "Do you feel older and more mature?" I ask her with a grin.

She grins back. "Older, yes. Mature? Never."

I'd told her to dress comfortably for our day of movie watching, so she's wearing pink and black striped leggings that do wonders to the curve of her ass, as well as a long sleeved Ivory Ella shirt with a cute cartoon image of an elephant on it. It's Keanna's new favorite clothing brand, because the company donates money to saving elephants. She only has one of their shirts right now because she discovered the company a month ago, but she'll have more when she opens my presents.

"So what movies did you get?" she asks as we walk from my back door toward the dining room.

"Mom picked them out, so don't worry," I say with a chuckle. "I think they'll be perfectly girly and romantic enough for you."

She gives me this bashful smile. "You'll like them too, Jett. Everyone loves romance."

I pretend to gag, just to keep up my manliness. She punches me in the stomach.

We find my family in the kitchen. "There's the birthday girl!" my mom says to Brooke in her baby voice. "Can you give Keanna a big birthday smile?"

Brooke grins easily, especially when you talk to her in a high pitched voice. Keanna gushes at the baby smile and she bends down and kisses Brooke's fat baby cheek. "Thank you, Brookie!" she says.

"What is she wearing?" I ask as I make baby faces at my little sister. Mom's dressed her in the fluffiest outfit on earth. A pink T-shirt with sparkles all over it, and pink leggings and this pink sparkly tutu thing around her waist. She's wearing socks that have both sparkles and like mini tutus around the ankles. Brooke's hair is covered in a sparkly headband with a flower and rhinestones on it.

Basically, my baby sister has been dunked in a bucket of pink sparkle.

"She's adorable," Mom says. "It's her party outfit."

"I love it," Keanna says. "You're the prettiest baby in the world!" Brooke squeals and holds Keanna's hand in her little baby fist.

"She can probably be seen from space," I say. "That's more sparkle than a craft store."

Dad laughs from the other side of the room, where

he's setting out tiny plates and forks. "Your mother never got to dress you up because boy clothes don't sparkle," he explains. "She's making up for that now."

"Damn right I am," Mom says. Brooke flails toward Keanna so Mom hands her over. "Jett's clothes were *so* boring when he was a baby. Oh my God. Monster trucks, monkeys, and alligators and stuff. No sparkle at all."

Keanna's smile is never as big as when she's holding her brother or my sister. Watching her play with the baby gives me all kinds of feelings that, as a guy, I usually try to ignore.

Like how one day if we have kids, she'll be that happy playing with them. I try to imagine being a parent. Taking care of a baby that's actually mine and not just my little sister. Raising a kid to know right from wrong, teaching them how to tie their shoes and cleaning up puke when they're sick. All the things my parents have done over the years.

It's a ton of work. I only like playing with Brooke when my parents are there to make sure I don't screw up. I can't even imagine doing it all alone, and that's exactly what my mom and dad did when they had me. They're my heroes. Someday, I hope Keanna and I will be half the parents they are.

My mom lights the candles on Keanna's cake and we

sing her happy birthday. She looks so beautiful sitting in front of the candles, her face glowing from the flames. I kind of wish everyone else would leave so I could be alone with her.

Brooke seems to love all of it, from the singing to the candles to the sound the wrapping paper makes as Keanna tears it off her gifts. My dad gives her a yearly membership to the local car wash place that Keanna loves. They wash your car as much as you want if you're a member. He also gets her one of those hard shell suit-cases for when we travel to races together. She'd been borrowing an old suitcase of mine before, but snow she has her own. She likes it so much, I worry she won't like my gift nearly as much as this one.

Mom gives her lots of clothes, all of which are things Keanna beams at and squeals over. While Mom and her are gushing over the clothes, which are apparently exactly what Keanna wanted, Dad and I exchange bored looks. He winks at me. "Get used to it, son. Your mom knows your girlfriend better than we do."

I laugh. "She hasn't seen my gift yet," I say, giving her a wink. "But you have to wait until we get upstairs to get it."

She grins at me.

We finish our cake and then my parents wish her happy birthday one last time before leaving to go next door. Keanna knows I've planned a movie day for us, but she doesn't know that I've transformed the game room into our own personal theater.

"Close your eyes," I say when we reach the top of the stairs. "And prepare to be amazed."

CHAPTER NINE

Keanna

I DON'T KNOW what I'm expecting when Jett tells me to close my eyes. Well, popcorn, I guess. I can smell it at the top of the stairs. Jett's hand closes around mine and I hear his crutches shuffling as he walks me to the game room.

"Okay, open your eyes."

I do, and I'm faced with a thick red curtain blocking the arched entryway to the game room. I lift an eyebrow. It's obviously a temporary addition to the house because the curtains have been thumbtacked into the wall.

Jett rolls out his hand and pushes it open for me.

"Welcome to the birthday theater," he says, then he frowns. "Okay that was lame. I should have thought of a better name."

I step into the game room and my mouth falls open. Jett's turned the space into a movie theater. It's dark in here, with all of the windows blocked out. White rope lighting is taped to the floor, forming a fake center aisle just like in the real movie theaters. It leads to a leather loveseat that's positioned in the middle of the room, right in front of a huge drop down movie screen that definitely wasn't there before today.

The other chairs in the room have been shoved off to the side, making it just a theater for two people: Jett and me.

On the back wall of the room, there's a real popcorn maker, filled up with freshly popped popcorn. There's even paper bags with red and white stripes and a little metal scoop to fill the bags just like at the movies. There's a table next to it with canned drinks in a bucket of ice, candy in dishes, and candy bars laid out—all of my favorites.

"You really outdid yourself," I say, grinning as I turn back to Jett.

He's leaning on his crutches, but he lowers his head down to mine as I wrap my arms around him. "Thank you."

"Happy Birthday," he says. "We get to spend the next eight hours watching romantic old movies on a ninety inch screen. And pigging out on junk food, of course."

"Is there any other way to spend a birthday?" I ask.

He grins. "Nope."

"Actually..." I say, sliding my fingers up Jett's hard chest. I peer up at him, letting my intentions be known with the look in my eyes. "I can think of a better way to spend our time. At least...before the first movie starts."

His eyes fill with desire, and a little grin appears on his lips. Balancing his crutches under his arms, he grabs my hips. "Oh yeah? Like what?"

I push him toward the loveseat, and he hobbles over. Even in crutches, Jett is the sexiest guy I know. His arm muscles only flex more on the crunches, the strength there turning me on. He eases himself into the loveseat and pats the seat next to him. I shake my head.

"That's not where I'm sitting," I say. I lower myself onto his lap.

"Mmm," he murmurs. His hands slide up my thighs. "I'm loving these leggings, by the way. You look sexy as hell in them."

"Does that mean you don't want me to take them off?" I say as I slide my hands up his shirt, then pull it over his head.

He smirks, his hands finding their way up my shirt to unhook my bra. "As sexy as they look on you, my love, they would definitely look better on the floor."

I pull off my shirt and Jett's mouth instantly goes to my breast. All thoughts leave my mind as his tongue flicks over my skin with expertise. I gasp and rock against him.

"I love you, baby doll," Jett breathes against my neck.

I tug on the button of his jeans. "Prove it."

Once our clothes are back on, and I'm feeling more loved than I thought possible, Jett and I settle into the temporary movie theater. I get us popcorn and candy and we snuggle up under the massive movie screen.

Maybe it's the sugar, or the salty popcorn, or the love of my favorite old school romances, but I feel my stress melt away. I'm here with Jett, wrapped in his strong arms and kept warm by a throw blanket, and Molly Ringwald is on the movie screen. School doesn't matter. Chores and work don't matter. Nothing all can weigh me down right in this moment. I am happy and free and relaxed.

Jett's phone vibrates as soon as the credits start to roll on the movie Sixteen Candles.

"Shit," he says as he leans over to take the phone out of his pocket. "I thought I turned this thing off."

"You can answer it," I say, getting up to stretch my limbs and get some more soda.

"It's Clay. I guess I should."

He answers the phone and I use the opportunity to go pee, then get more drinks and candy. When Jett finishes with the short phone call, he smiles up at me.

"Clay won this weekend's race," he says, taking the Dr. Pepper I hand him. "Team Loco is officially winning more arenacross races than any other team."

"That's good, right?" I sit next to him, placing the bag of popcorn between us.

He nods. "If it's not me winning, I at least want it to be one of my teammates."

I get up to put the next movie into the DVD player and settle back next to Jett, which could otherwise be called the greatest place on earth to sit. I love the smell of his cologne. The taste of his lips (salty and buttery from the popcorn) as we kiss every so often. I love everything about him.

"I love that you're here with me," I say, leaning my head against his shoulder. "This is the best birthday ever."

"Oh shit," Jett says, sitting up. "I totally forgot to give you your present! It's over there on the other couch." He nods toward the couch that's up against the wall, then he pushes up on his hands and reaches for his crutches.

"Don't worry about it," I say, putting my arm over his. "Just stay here with me. I'm comfortable."

"But it's your birthday present," he says. "You're going to love it."

"I know I will," I say, snuggling my head against his chest. "I'll get it later. For now, I just want to enjoy all this time with you."

He laughs and runs his fingers through my hair, before resting his cheek on top of my head. "You're the birthday girl," he says. "So I'll do as you say."

CHAPTER
TEN

Jett

SILVER COUNTY MEDICAL smells like plastic and rubbing alcohol. The fluorescent lights are too bright and the staff is too cheery for this early in the morning. I yawn and cover my mouth with my hand. The paper cover of the exam bed crinkles under my weight.

In the chair across from me sits my girlfriend, her head resting in her hand. She's exhausted too. We probably shouldn't have stayed up all night last night binge watching Netflix, but what's done is done. The Flash is a pretty damn good show and we couldn't stop watching it even though we knew I had a 9 a.m. doctor appointment this morning.

There's a knock on the door and then the doctor comes in. He's young, probably fresh out of medical school, and he's smiling brightly as if he did the responsible thing and got plenty of sleep last night. "Ready to get this cast off?" he asks.

"Hell yes I am."

The doctor uses a cast saw thing, which I've seen a dozen times in my life, but it's new to Keanna.

"Is that a saw?" she asks, eyes wide in fear.

"Kind of," the doctor says, showing it to her. "The blade isn't sharp by itself. It vibrates very quickly and that's what cuts off the cast. It won't cut skin."

He turns it on and touches it to the back of his hand, and sure enough, there's no cut underneath the blade. Keanna lifts an eyebrow, but doesn't look very convinced as she leans forward in her chair, biting on her bottom lip.

The doctor cuts into the side of my cast, and the vibrations tickle a little. My skin is warm where the saw cuts through the cast, but it doesn't hurt. Soon, he's halfway down and then he starts up the other side.

"You'll need to take it easy," he warns me as he works the saw through the cast. "Your leg won't be back to one hundred percent for a couple of weeks."

"It's all good," I say, glancing at Keanna who is looking very concerned at my leg. "I'll take December off and then get back to the winter series that kicks off in January."

The cast is pried off my leg, revealing one pasty ass white appendage that doesn't match my other one at all. My leg hair is all matted up and my ankle is weak, but I can move it. Finally.

"Freedom!" I say, pumping my fist in the air.

Keanna rolls her eyes. The doctor laughs, and finishes his examination.

When it's time for me to stand on my own two feet for the first time in forever, Keanna rushes to my side, throwing my arm around her shoulders. She's so cute and loving and caring and I think I might explode from the warm fuzzy feeling it gives me.

We walk down the hallway and back up again, much slower than I'd like, but it's something. I'm walking again. I'm no longer relying to Crutchy to get me places.

Keanna drives us home in her Mustang, and I spend the entire ride home moving my ankle up and down and back and forth. I missed being able to do this. Also, I am in serious need of a tan from the knee down. Now that it's almost winter, I won't be wearing shorts much so this ungodly uneven tan I have will probably last until spring.

My parents are having lunch with Keanna's parents, and they brought the babies with them, so we're all alone.

Keanna insists on keeping her arm around my waist as we walk into my house. I'm a little weak, sure, but I'm fine. Still, I hold onto her shoulders and let her help me because she cares so much and I'm so grateful to have a girl like her on my side, looking after me. I've heard all kinds of stories in my life about how motocross girl-friends tend to dump a guy when he's no longer winning races. Keanna isn't like that, not one bit.

"So what do you want to do with your newfound leg freedom?" she asks me as she pours us a cup of sweet tea.

I sit on the barstool and consider it for a moment. "I want to get on my bike," I say, and that earns me a quick glare from my girlfriend. I laugh. "I know I can't do that right now, so I think I'll go for the next best thing."

Keanna leans on the kitchen island, her elbows squeezing her boobs together as she takes a sip of her tea. "What's that?"

I grin. "Take a shower. A real one. Standing up in the hot water with my leg *not* wrapped in a freaking trash bag."

She laughs. "Probably a good idea. It's no telling how bad your leg smells right now."

I use the handrail to help me hobble up the stairs,

and by the time I'm in my room, Keanna is already in my bathroom, running the hot water.

"Baby," I say, leaning against the bathroom door frame. "I love you so much, but when you do all these things for me, I feel bad.'

"Why would you feel bad?" she asks, setting a clean towel on the towel rack for me. "I'm just helping. I'm happy to do it."

"I know. But you don't have to do those things. I should be doting on you."

"It's a two-way street," she says, pressing her hands flat on my chest as she leans up and kisses me. "I'm happy to do things for you."

She starts to step away and I stop her with a hook of my hand around her back. I tug her close and kiss her on the lips, harder than I mean to. She sighs against me, her body pressing all up against mine. Her breasts feel amazing, and I can't help but picture what they'd feel like if there weren't shirts in between us.

The shower fogs up the air around us, casting a steamy glow on the mirror.

"I need your help with one more thing," I whisper into her ear.

"What's that?" she says, giving me this adorably not-so-innocent look.

"It's been a while since I showered without a cast on

my leg." I slide my finger down her side and up again. "I think I might need some help."

Her cheeks turn pink and then she gives me a sultry look, as if she's already undressing me with her eyes. "Like I said earlier," she says as she slides her hands up under my shirt and lifts it over my head. "I'm happy to help."

ABOUT THE AUTHOR

Amy Sparling is the *USA Today* bestselling author of books for teens and the teens at heart. A librarian by day, she lives on the coast of Texas with her family, her spoiled rotten pets, and a huge pile of books. Her favorite things are coffee, book boyfriends, and Netflix binges. You can also find her writing books for Young Adults and Middle Schoolers under the name Cheyanne Young.